PURPOSE:

This book was written for anyone, whether a Christian or even an atheist, who would like to have a better life.

I hope you enjoy this most relatable, entertaining story; and more importantly, that you will apply these **Three Priceless Techniques.** They will help you to effortlessly free yourself of limiting beliefs, negative emotional states, and transform every area of your life!

You can easily read this book in under two hours. Some readers choose to read it a little bit at a time. Most readers re-read it many times, as there tends to be an *experience* each time. Many are calling **Christ's Castle** - *The Experience Book.*

"Daniel, what a phenomenal book! I so enjoyed the story and the teachings. The Three Priceless Techniques that you describe (and show how to use in our everyday lives) are so powerful that I am incorporating them into my own practice. What a gift you have written for humanity, as it will change how people look at themselves and the world. You will know you are different and transformed from the minute you wake up in the morning. Thank you, thank you!!!"
--Dr. Eric Robins, co-author of Your Hands Can Heal You

"This book is an inspiring and delightful tool for daily practices. It teaches simple techniques that today's humanity needs to deal with their day-to-day challenges. It is also a great beginning to understand suffering and connect with your inner Christ" - **Sri Madhuji**

"Daniel O'Hara brings joy, inspiration and uniqueness to this spiritual journey of wisdom that will touch, heal and uplift the young and old alike. A must read!"- **Kim Somers Egelsee, #1 best-selling author of Getting Your Life to a 10+**

"Daniel's Christ's Castle is such a relatable story. An investment of an hour will pay dividends for the rest of your life!" – **Loren Slocum, CEO of Lobella Int'l and author Life Tuneups: Your Personal Plan to Find Balance, Discover Your Passion, and Step into Greatness**

"Daniel has written an "old soul" book. It's full of ancient wisdom, but it's exceptionally applicable in the modern world. It's evolved, practical and easy-to-use." - **John Merryman, co-author Your Hands Can Heal You**

There's a volcano's worth of energy, power, light, and transformation inside this little book! - **Karen Rauch Carter, author of Move Your Stuff, Change Your Life and Make a Shift, Change Your Life**

Christ's Castle: Three Priceless Techniques to Transform Your Life!

(Book One in the Christ's Castle Series)

By Daniel O'Hara

Copyright © 2018 by Daniel O'Hara

This book and other titles and videos can be found at:

www.DanielOHara.com

Printed in the U.S.A

CHRIST'S CASTLE

Three Priceless Techniques to Transform Your Life!

(Book One in the Christ's Castle Series)

by

Daniel O'Hara

The Crisis

My hands were shaking... My head was pounding as if Mike Tyson was continually beating on it. With each punch came more damage and trauma. While earlier in the day I had delivered the presentation of my life, and literally wowed the conference room; this simply didn't matter anymore. One of the greatest achievements in my career was now a distant memory. I was overwhelmed with a huge predicament and didn't know how to get out of it. My evening had turned into a nightmare...

The day started off great and festivities were planned for the evening. Eve and I were celebrating our thirteenth wedding anniversary along with our son Allen's eighth birthday. The house felt airy and joy-filled. There was a special indescribable happiness - a palpable feeling of benevolence.

At work, I delivered the presentation of my life. It was in front of the Board, the Executive Management team and most of the company. The CEO/President of the company, my biggest fan, loved it! My team loved it! My direct superior however, did not! The attention I received from the CEO/President brought out the dark side of my direct superior, Jackson. Jackson, while overall a good guy, still had some character flaws. Most of my co-workers loved it; however, there were still some that took it as a personal threat to their positions. Tonight, none of these workplace events mattered. It was all about our son.

It was 5:30 PM, and my life had suddenly become *surreal*. We were preparing for our Anniversary and Allen's Birthday revelries for the evening. I was getting ready to leave, so I could watch the end of Allen's football practice, when I received a call on my cell from a number I didn't recognize. Still buzzing in preparation for the night at hand and post-bliss of the events of the day, I cheerfully answered.

After a quick obligatory "Hello," the caller frantically attempted to put words together. It was Allen's coach. As the coach blurted, "The ambulance is on its way," these words made the one hundred trillion cells in my body tremble with concern for my progeny. I had great difficulty trying to come up with words to respond and doled out, "Huh?" Regaining my senses, I immediately queried, "What…What happened?"

The coach proceeded to explain that Allen was making a tackle, and he incorrectly put his head down resulting in a concussion. He was now unconscious. The ambulance and paramedics had just arrived. They were examining him now. I was to meet them at the hospital. I was immediately propelled into a mental and emotional fog. I felt as if I was floating on a small boat in the middle of the ocean with no clue as to the whereabouts of land and/or direction. It was so *surreal*.

Entering the emergency room doors, my body was now fueled with adrenaline. This fuel gave me the energy to cope with the current situation but helped to inflame the tension in my neck and shoulders. Mentally, I was unclear, and my emotions were a cocktail of uncertainty - two-parts concern and one-part hope that everything would be okay. Once through security, I found hallways of people in a world of organized chaos. Allen's room was the last door at the end of the longest hall. There was a small gaggle of nurses and doctors examining him. After maybe fifteen minutes (of what seemed like hours), from what I could gather from their conversation, they were going to do more evaluations including a CAT Scan, an MRI and an overnight stay for observation.

Allen was soon *gurnied* to another room that was even more impersonal and almost vault-like. Through a small window, I could see Allen from a distance. Watching him through a looking glass in the waiting room made me feel more like a distant observer than a concerned parent. The CAT Scan machine entwined Allen like a giant, metallic cobra grasping his body and swallowing his head.

Was this whole experience *real*, a dream or rather, just a nightmare? "If it was just a nightmare, PLEASE, wake me up," I mentally pleaded. Or, worse yet, was this some sort of punishment? I'd never really done anything bad in my life, or at least so I thought. When I was young, I was a self-absorbed idiot and I acted like most kids during my teenage years – unaware and with selfish intentions. While I wasn't a saint by any stretch, I certainly never tried to hurt other people. This internal dialogue was circling in my head from the adrenaline dump. As the adrenaline started wearing off, my body told my mind it needed a chair, so I sat down.

My physical body was tired, my brain still continued thinking, albeit at a slower pace, on its own. Perhaps it was the last bits of adrenaline hitting the cerebral cortex. "Was our son going to be OK? Was he going to have brain damage? Was he going to be paralyzed? Was he ever going to be the same strong, fun loving kid?" were questions that revealed themselves due to the fragile nature of the situation at hand.

"Surely, there was a better way?" I questioned. My thoughts continued, "Was there some sort of salvation to this suffering? Oh God, please help!" Almost screaming in my mind… "Please help! There must be a better way of living my life without all this suffering. I'm so tired of the pain and the pain I see in the world." While today was extraordinary, most days were a struggle, and tonight was just too much to bear.

This inner dialogue of requesting help, surrender or whatever it was called; was very foreign to me. While sitting, or rather due to my tiredness, now reclining uncomfortably in the hospital chair, I closed my eyes and started drifting off to sleep…

The Dream

Most nights, it took some time for me to fall asleep. I often resorted to taking a drink, reading a book, or ingesting an over-the-counter sleeping pill for any hope of rapid slumber. I was one of the 48% of people in America who suffered from insomnia. Needing something external to help me fall asleep and to break the monotonous routine of lying sleepless, I would sometimes add one of those *plop, plop, fizz, fizz* things to a glass of water. It was also supposed to help with sinuses, which also bothered me. I believed, "Why not accomplish both at the same time?"

Watching the white wafer hit the water was like watching a mini-explosion with an accompanying fizz sound. While it didn't completely knock me out, it was good for a little bit of tension relief. The commercial used to chime "Oh, what a relief it is...," and this jingle played in my head each time. Tonight, for a change, an external substance, or bedtime ritual wasn't needed. The roller coaster of emotional highs and lows of the day had finally fatigued my poor body and mind. This fatigue created an easy transition from consciousness to sleep.

Unaware that I was now sleeping, I found myself in a dream. While awake, the physical world seemed *real.* However, this dream world seemed to be even more *real.* "How could this be even more *real*?" I thought.

From the darkness, a golden orb of light appeared, moving ever closer into my awareness. Its emergence from total darkness jolted my already *realer* feeling to an even more intensified state.

The bright orb now visible to my closed, *inner* eyes morphed into the Christ. In this particular dream, the colors were more vibrant, and the sensations were more experiential. "Joe," the Christ said as he sat leaning next to me, "The life you wished for when you fell asleep *is possible; it does exist!*"

I was clearly hearing the words of the Christ speaking to me, as if it was *realer* than a conversation with another human. "What in the world?" I deliberated.

The Christ continued, "While you think this physical world you live in is real, it is merely an illusion. It is an illusion within your mind…"

Never having a frame of reference for such an experience, I was wondering what was happening. This was the first time I had ever had such a vivid and real encounter or let alone a dream like this before. I immediately asked, "Why are you here?" Before providing the Christ an opportunity to respond, I continued and blurted out, "Why are you helping *me?"*

The Christ smiled. With a grace and tone unlike any other, he shared, "Because, you asked." He said he was moved by my deep desire to get out of misery, and his compassionate nature allowed him to intervene when genuine cries for help warranted it. "Joe, you have the ability to get out of suffering."

I now paused for a moment, a rarity for me, and took in what he said. As if he was reading my mind, I was wondering if I could ever get out of this hamster wheel of pain and suffering only to be followed up with more anguish.

"The problem is with your over identification of the transitory world around you, Joe. You believe your world is real. It is an illusion. In Hebrew, the world you see with your physical eyes, the world of illusion is called *Mamlakah* הָכָלְמַמ. In Aramaic is it called *Malkuth* מלכות. Since you are so caught up in the mode of survival, your ego, your emotions and beliefs; your inner peace, or heaven is rarely experienced. In Romans 12:2 it says, "And do not imitate this world, but be transformed by the renovation of your minds, and you shall distinguish what is the good, acceptable and perfect will of God."

While he was speaking and even while I was in a dream, I sensed something inside me was changing. My body felt less stress and lighter, almost weightless. For much of my life, I had always felt reactive and defensive. There had been many times that my life was filled with high hopes of a glorious outcome, whether it be financial, work-related, or with my home-life; only to have something bad occur at the last minute. The last *eleventh hour* of disappointments sent my emotions spiraling out of control only to be followed by a crash landing. Needless to say, I usually reacted harshly, negatively, and self-destructively after these setbacks.

This internal feeling of *lightness* was gaining momentum, as I started feeling yet another round of improvement. Rather than feeling my standard defensive and guarded response, which made me feel heavy and congested; I was now feeling an ability to be proactive. This feeling of being proactive gave me hope that I might be able to create the reality with which the Christ was so eloquently speaking. In some indiscernible way, I intuitively knew what was happening... His gracious presence initiated a *domino effect* that let me see my life from a different perspective, and that my physical illusion *was* changing. I felt I had a better handle on this whole experience. "Of course, this whole thing was a dream, and maybe I was just deluding myself," I inwardly chuckled to myself. If I was chuckling during this time of crisis, maybe this whole dream was *real* after all?!

He remained sitting patiently looking at me, so I decided to ask another question, "How can I change it - this *Malkuth* thing - the illusion I mean?"

The Christ smiled and said, "Joe, it is really very easy! I will teach you **Three Priceless Techniques.** The more you apply these **Techniques** in your daily life, the easier they will become, and the less stressful your life will be. Your life will have much more peace, meaning, ease, and you'll help those around you, as well."

I was dubious, but captivated. "I really had the power to change myself and those who surround me? And, with only **Three Techniques?"** I mulled it over and wanted to hear more. Yet, a part of me was still feeling reluctant to change and was skeptical. While the way I lived my life was probably killing me at an ever-accelerated rate, it was my routine. It was all I knew, and I had never been very good at adopting new routines.

The Christ continued, "Not only will these **Techniques** help you and your life, but these **Techniques** will help magnetize others to do the same. As more people do them, you and others will have the power to transform the world into a giant *Christ's Castle*."

"*Christ's Castle…* What is a *Christ's Castle?*" I asked.

"Good question," the pleased Christ replied. "I'll explain that in a moment. But first, in order for you to understand where you are going, we need to review where you've been!"

The Review

With a whoosh, the Christ and I seemed to be sitting on balcony with a canopy. From this *Christ Canopy* perspective, we looked down and saw my bedroom with my body sleeping in bed.

It was a Monday morning and a little after sunrise. I watched as I slammed the off button on my digital alarm clock, a bit harder than intended, and the clock slid a few inches on the nightstand. We watched my head fall back onto my pillow and my eyes close again. I drew in a quick, somewhat tense breath and appeared to brace myself for the new day. I watched myself attempting to get out of bed. I didn't look happy. The king-sized bed was empty on the other side. Eve had been up long enough that her side was cold.

Monday mornings seemed to worsen with the sound of an electronic, buzzing alarm clock. "Why do companies make clocks with such irritating alarms? Why start the day off irritated?" I deliberated to myself. "One of these days I should get an alarm connected to my iPhone and play U2's *Beautiful Day* upon waking. At least that song would inspire happy thoughts and set a much better tone for the day." I wondered if I was the only one to think such thoughts, as I watched my body slowly roll out of bed. With heavy feet and sleepy guck in my eyes, my body lumbered to the bathroom.

I was slightly sad watching this daily ritual of waking, and I looked to the Christ for comfort and guidance. Not changing his facial expression in any way, his gentle smile oozed with peace, and that smile gave me some modicum of reassurance of a better life.

My entry into the shower marked my favorite part of each morning. Three to five minutes of peace before the mundane drudgery and conflict in my daily life would begin. There was something delightful about the caress of the water upon my skin that not only washed off my body, but also seemed to revitalize and nurture my soul - whatever that meant . . .

"Perhaps it simply felt good to do something that was directed purely for my rejuvenation? Maybe it was the comfort of a morning ritual, like a knight donning his armor? Whatever it was, I told myself that I was better not to over-analyze it and ruin the moment because the moment was feeling good," I counseled myself. I rationalized that too much thinking was like playing your favorite album too many times. Over the years, I annoyed my family on many occasions by playing a song over and over again. Maybe I should stop replaying thoughts in my head and irritating myself, as well.

The Christ looked at me watching this shower scene play out without saying anything, yet his look appeared to confirm that my shower dialogue was right.

"Wow," I thought, "I'm conversing with a Christ in a dream and watching myself in a shower. And, while I'm in the shower, I'm thinking, and now the Christ is complimenting me... Whoa... There are a lot of levels to this. I have a lot to learn," I reflected to myself. As these new realizations revealed themselves, my jaw was starting to relax, and a warm smile emerged, as I stood on the *Christ Canopy.*

Emerging from the shower, a fragment of a scene played in my mind's eye. It was an image from the same elusive dream that I had been having over years. I felt peaceful, saw an outline of something divine, and then poof it was gone!

I exchanged a few brief words with my wife Eve about her plans for the day. Between getting herself ready each morning and getting the kids rushed off to school, the conversation was always hasty and incomplete. Most of the time, she was rushing around hurriedly. With her attention in many directions, I was challenged in hearing her words correctly. This inability to hear her clearly, aggravated me to no end. It seemed that she always turned her head away from me on the key word in a sentence. Not hearing that key word allowed for several interpretations in her sentence. While many husbands might not have cared about what their wife had to say, I cared what she had to say. I wished that she was more composed, relaxed, and was able to look at me when she was speaking. Maybe, it was too much to ask given all of her responsibilities with the kids, home and work? I remembered a bumper sticker I once saw, *the best gift you can give someone is your presence.*

Conversations with Eve were more productive and harmonious later in the evening, after nine to be more specific. Although we were both tired at the end of the day, at least we weren't rushing around, and could speak in the same room without anyone else vying for our attention. I looked forward to these less intense moments, but it seemed that those times were growing fewer with each passing year.

This time when I looked over at the Christ, I was embarrassed by my aggravation with Eve. She was so busy, and who was I to judge her? I certainly wasn't perfect. And besides, to be aggravated by her working so hard for our family was really pretty immature, I realized.

The Christ maintained his smile as if to say, "Very good!" The Christ showed me these scenes as if we were watching a movie together. I was the lead character in this drama. A drama it was, and there was way too much drama!

A drama that proved pretty saddening. Watching myself as a spectator helped me a great deal. As I watched, I was able to be an observer which gave me a new perspective. I was more detached as I could see how I was entangled in the barbed tentacles of my own emotions, thoughts and beliefs. These tentacles were like a huge Squid drowning me. I remembered a National Geographic episode that I watched about the Colossal Squid, and how their tentacles had suckers with rotating hooks inside them. Their arms would hold their victim, the rotating hooks which were inside their suckers would slice the flesh and break into the meat of their victim then into the squid's beak or mouth. Recalling the rotating hooks made my *mental movie* even scarier. I started reflecting on how poorly I started off my day, and more importantly, how many flaws I had. I now saw these flaws as hooks.

Again, without changing his demeanor or expression, the Christ gave me his consistent smile of support. I sensed his confirmation that I was finally getting it, and we quickly transitioned to the next part of the day.

We moved to a scene at the breakfast table. From the *Christ Canopy* I watched as I munched sullenly on my breakfast. The brown cereal and brown toast seemed like a metaphor for the tone my day would be, nothing but life depleting brown... As I read the paper, I saw many conflicts. Murders, military skirmishes, children developing autism, crooked politicians, GMOs in our food supply, and a local company CEO caught lying to its shareholders filled the front pages. "Why was there so much suffering in the world?" I quixotically reflected.

In the background, our kids were starting off the day with their own mini-version of global conflict; fighting over the cable remote control and which channel to watch.

"I want to watch *Sponge Bob*!" yelled my son Allen. "NO! I want to watch *Powder Puff Girls*!" shouted Amy, the younger of the two.

From my position on the sidelines, I saw how, even in the early stages of childhood, there seemed to be an inherent tendency towards conflict. And, it appeared from reading the paper, it only progressed and worsened as we become adults, I surmised.

It was *surreal* to be with the Christ, again watching myself experience *my* day. While watching my review, I was able to feel the stress of the day and hear my own internal dialogue. The most beneficial part was examining these very thoughts, emotions and encounters with the enlightening, gracious presence of the Christ. Having him *over my shoulder* watching my reactions to these scenes helped me improve my awareness. I surveyed many blocks on my road of life. Some of the blocks were like giant boulders, lodged in potholes on my highway to becoming a better person.

The Review of the Drive

While going to work and likely for most people, I habitually found the transition from our home to my car somewhat depressing. It was as if I was compartmentalizing from our humble home into a small metal box with wheels. From one box providing my body a place to rest to a smaller box that provided my body transportation. Once at work, I would further compartmentalize again into a cubicle. I was fortunate that I had worked my way up to my own office, which made the whole *compartmentalizing* process a little more palatable.

As I pulled out of the driveway, the car stereo came on with two local DJs, who made the tedious drive to work a little more bearable. I listened to their show every morning during the workweek. I noticed a pattern in their intention to laugh approximately every 22 seconds. Counting to 22 and listening for their conjured laughter actually made me chuckle. The topics of their jokes consisted of the usual: men, women, body parts, relationships, bosses, current news, celebrities, and of course the easiest and best target, politicians.

Making my way through rush hour traffic on the highway, I wondered how long it would take for another car to cut me off. The drive on the 404 freeway each morning was no treat. I could get to my office in only fifteen minutes if it wasn't for the traffic, but instead it usually took 45-50 minutes.

Slamming my right foot onto the brake, the event I anticipated suddenly occurred. Being cutoff in traffic was almost similar to the consistency of fake laughter by the morning DJs. Another driver in a new Porsche cut me off. He would have hit my car had it not been for my anticipation of his actions and having decent reflexes. The rude driver raised his hand in the air at me while looking in his rear-view mirror, as if to say I was at fault. The audacity of him blaming me granted me the license to fly off the handle and retort. So, I mouthed clearly, "You're an asshole!" so that he could read my lips while he was looking back at me.

I remembered reading about two guys yelling at each other on the freeway which resulted in a shooting and a death. The news was filled with events like this. I thought this was so pointless. Fighting over inconsequential space on a freeway was moronic. My heart was racing after this experience, and my body grew tenser. The day was still so young, and I was already beginning to feel old and tired . . . "If I felt this way at only 35," I said to myself, "How old would I feel like when I was 45 or 55?"

I looked over at the Christ. By just turning and looking to him, I didn't need to say anything. It was clear - I acted like an ass. Who was I to be so negative to people? And, what a waste of energy! It started becoming clear to me. I was directing negative energy to this random guy on the highway. In fact, while I re-watched this scene again, for a microsecond, I thought I saw red energy being hurled back and forth. We were throwing prickly fireballs at each other, and they were hitting our heads, hearts and solar plexus. I started questioning, "Maybe the other guy had so much on his mind that he didn't mean to cut me off? What if I truly wasn't giving him enough space on the freeway? Maybe he just lost his job, his girlfriend, or something even worse?" I now felt sorry for the poor guy and even more disappointed in myself for being so ignorant.

The Christ and I reviewed my morning thus far from the start of my day at home to the eventful drive to work. Having done this twice now, I was starting to see a pattern emerge. I certainly wasn't proud of what I saw. My emotions and thoughts had continued to escalate with each situation. I would find fault in others and

continually made myself right. It was like the kindling of an inner fire. These increasingly negative emotions were the sparks that ignited the kindling of my negative thoughts. When combined, they would explode into an out-of-control inferno. This inferno would then be projected to others. "Maybe, this type of behavior would lead me one day to *Dante's Inferno*," I pondered.

Maybe to bring myself solace, or out of concern for the well-being of others, I started to wonder if others felt this way too? Surely, I wasn't the only one... We continued into another review session.

The Review of Work

Arriving at the office five minutes late only intensified the stress and duress of my morning. Clocking in on my computer always bothered me. It felt like the company was attaching a shackle to my leg. In a way, it was like a physical shackle, as if I was tethered to my desk. It was also like a mental shackle, since the company owned my mental productivity during business hours. I took pride in doing my job well and maximizing my time. It felt uncomfortable logging in late, even though it was only a few minutes. Or, maybe it was just nagging memories of my mother reminding me to be early. Either way, being late only elevated my stress.

I looked over at the Christ. While he always maintained his countenance, I sensed he acknowledged what I was thinking. As I watched the scenes playout, I could feel my stress deepen, like an unholy cocktail of chemicals being distributed into my veins. It was early in the day and I was already on my third cup of coffee to keep my energy level up. Despite my flawed habits, the Christ was still smiling. Although he didn't physically move his eyes or lips, I could swear he squinted his eyes and smiled with pride that I was understanding this deeper way of connecting and learning from my experiences.

As the National Director of Sales, I needed to be a great example to my team. The sales representatives, who reported to me were already clamoring for my attention and asking questions. I found it particularly annoying when they repeatedly asked the same questions. My usual facial expressions to them were evident that they should already know the answer which led me to more exasperation.

One of my reps, Michelle Hoops, was quite the character. She had more frenetic energy than anyone I had ever met. While she only drank one cup of coffee in the morning, it seemed like she had five or six shots of espresso. Not spending much time with people that did drugs regularly, I often wondered if she was on something. She was a relatively attractive blonde in her early 40's, and she could talk a mile a minute. Literally, if her mouth was timed, it could compete against the speed of a hummingbird's wings.

She would listen to my advice for about an hour, and then go back to her unproductive work habits, emailing prospective clients instead of calling them. "Had technology moved us beyond our personal relationships and exclusively to digital communication?" In this case, it was just her fear of not being good enough to sell on the phone. I often observed that fear was a major destroyer of capable salespeople. And, probably not just salespeople, but with people in all aspects of life.

Later in the day, I had to attend a sales meeting headed by the company's Vice President, Jackson Jones. Jackson had a short, stocky build. For the most part, he was a pretty good guy, except he had a Napoleon complex that overtook his goodness. He wanted everyone to know he was the boss, so much so, that he wanted all of us to call him Mr. Jones. He liked the sound of that, especially since our job was to make him more money.

His primary motivation was furthering his reputation with the CEO/President. He even said and maybe it was a Freudian slip, "He didn't have any friends because all he did was work." All of his interactions with us centered around talking about how close he was to the CEO. Since we weren't his friends, we were all just Jackson's subjects.

My position as National Sales Director was challenging. I was always torn between trying to do what was right for my reps, the company, and me. I often felt like a juggler with three balls to keep in the air. Having only two hands and no training in juggling, this regularly left one ball falling to the floor. There was, of course, a fourth ball, the clients. My family wasn't even considered in this part of the juggling act, adding ball number five. And, of course, this resulted in more balls succumbing to the effects of gravity.

After seeing my patterns of judging others, getting irritated over their interactions, and fueling the fires with my negative emotions, I once again looked over to the Christ in hopes for some sort of grace. This time I smiled at him as if to say, "I get it!" My internal process of feeling less stress while my body was feeling *lighter* was gaining momentum, and I was hopeful.

While at the meeting, I watched my body rocking back and forth. As my body moved, the chair squeaked, revealing my desire and readiness to leave. And...the meeting had just started. Fortunately for me, this weekly sales meeting went rather quickly with little interaction between the attendees, also known as *Jackson's subjects.* While I was a little uncertain whether Jackson cared for us individually, he absolutely cared for us *collectively*. His management style was more dictatorial. He wanted things done his way, and if you came up with a great idea; our CEO would hear about it as Jackson's idea. The other sales managers were uninspired by Jackson's guidance and the direction he was yet again taking the company.

I sat morosely in my chair as good ole Jennifer Cassidy began to shower Jackson with profuse compliments and use words like "brilliant" and "incredible!" Jennifer was a fiery, Irish woman. I began to think, that if she had kids, maybe it would have softened her stone-cold heart and ruthless ways. Her business life was all that she had. While Jackson was on a quest to only care what the CEO thought, Jennifer was on her own personal quest for power. She would do whatever it took to succeed. We used to joke around that she would even resort to *black magic* if it would help her career. While she would *brown nose* Jackson in the meetings and effuse him with compliments, she complained about him behind his back. I always wondered if she was complaining in order to fit in, and was conning us just like she conned Jackson?

At nearly every meeting, Jennifer would rush into the room to stake out her chair. She positioned herself next to Jackson every time. Surely, her kissing up would be obvious to Jackson; however, he never seemed to tire of it, or catch on for that matter. He appeared only to revel in it. He preferred hearing the ideas of women, rather than mine or the other men on the team. It appeared that his Napoleonic complex liked the attention of women and thwarted off any male competition.

I was one of the strongest players on the team and carried respect from the group - he especially didn't care for my input. In previous meetings when I offered input, it was quickly shot down. Occasionally, he'd offer me a flippant compliment on my idea, but it never really seemed sincere or go anywhere. While it was clear to everyone that the CEO believed in me and really treasured me, I hadn't felt support in many years from Jackson. I served the company for nearly a dozen years, and Jackson seemed to turn my successes into his own. Worse, over time, he just took me for granted. And, as far as promotions go, that was never going to happen for me.

"Maybe the problem with Jackson and I was primarily with me," I thought to myself. "Maybe it was predominantly my fault? I started thinking if the problem was just with me, than there wouldn't have been similar problems with Jackson and many others. I did a quick review over the dozen years. Many others had left the company as they felt taken advantage of by Jackson. Despite the fact that they worked hard for the company, they felt used by Jackson to advance his career and ending up leaving as well. Since I was one of the original members of management, and one of the last still surviving, the source of the problem was clearly Jackson. Too many have left, having their blood, sweat and tears poured into their territories only to be stolen by Jackson. Jackson was clearly the problem.

As the meeting concluded, Jackson asked me to stay behind in the conference room. One of our clients had complained about one of my sales reps, and it was my job to smooth the situation over. I was to call the client, be apologetic, calm the situation down, and afterward apply the appropriate disciplinary action to the sales rep. This whole process was taking a toll on me. It was as if I was a tank of fuel, and these little quarrels poked a tiny hole in my gas tank. The gas was trickling out, slowly at first, then gradually leaking more and more. Watching my body walk out of the meeting, my gait was considerably slower. I dreaded these talks with my reps. It was like babysitting them on a daily basis.

While I watched the scenes with the Christ by my side, there may have been some merit to my opinions of co-workers, but I was clearly judging them. I judged Jackson on his Napoleonic complex and judged Jennifer as a power hungry, evil witch. And, while she might have even engaged in *black magic* to advance her career, I was directing negative energy towards her just by seeing her this way. The sad part is, Jackson, or as we were supposed to refer to him as Mr. Jones, and I *could* have been great friends had there not been such a pedestal between us.

As I watched myself leave the office and head back to my car, it was clear I was readying myself for the ride home. Just as I closed my door and turned my car on, my cell phone rang. Abruptly, I fumbled around trying to get my earphone in my ear, while simultaneously trying to swipe my card to open the parking garage gate. Doing these three things at once was a recipe for failure. It intensified the feelings that my life was out of control. As I was taking too long in my exit out of the parking garage, I heard a honk from one of the cars behind me. Getting out of the garage at 5:05 PM was a competitive sport.

Finally, with my earphone successfully in, I was able to address the call. It was my mom calling with something that was very important in *her* world. While major to her, it was an activity that didn't need to be addressed for another month. I quickly closed the conversation and commenced my way to the busy on-ramp. I looked over at the Christ with chagrin on my face at the heartlessness I had just displayed to my mom. While it was certainly no excuse, it seemed that people like myself who tried to be nice to people, weren't necessarily the nicest to the people that were closest to them. This infinite revelation was shown in the eyes of the smiling Christ as if to say, "You are learning a great deal, and we'll cover this topic in the future…let's continue to review your day."

The Review of the Supermarket

The drive home after work was a repeat of the morning. As usual, I was cut off a couple of times. I, however, was just too tired to give much of a response in these instances. It appeared that this time my tiredness left me apathetic, which was probably better than hostile and warring. The gas out of my imaginary *gas tank* was leaking even more now.

I was making record time on my drive home and was only about four minutes away. I smiled thinking I'm almost there; until my cell phone rang again. It was my wife Eve, asking me to pick up donuts for our son's school function in the morning. Irritated at the request, I quickly and haughtily agreed. My mind was flooded with "Why didn't she do this during day," "She could have easily have done it," and "She knows the store way better than I do." From the *Christ Canopy* I watched myself having this imaginary conversation with her. I could see dark energetic squiggles and patterns forming around my head.

I continued on with my mental filibuster saying "It is going to take forever to find the donuts. The store is going to be ridiculously crowded," and "I'm going to miss the kickoff!" I thought I'd surely miss the first few minutes of *Monday Night Football*, which was a bright spot in my otherwise dull week. The classic *Monday Night Football Theme Song* reminded me of my deceased father and the memories we had watching the game together. The song was always good for a few endorphins.

At the store, I tried to call Eve, but was unsuccessful. "Why is it that cell phones will work in parking structures, even elevators, but not this supermarket?" I agonizingly questioned. I again used my logic to exacerbate my negative emotional state. I could feel my temples tighten and my ears get warm, as my blood-pressure elevated. My visualization of not being able to find the donuts was correct... I walked down a few aisles without any success.

From our view on the *Christ Canopy,* I quickly considered that maybe my *visualizations* were creating my negative reality. With a whoosh, I was back watching the scene, not needing confirmation or a reply from the Christ. I was learning and understanding at a much quicker pace now.

Since I couldn't find the donuts on my own, I needed to find a box-boy or a clerk. It took another five minutes to find someone who could help. This was their busiest time of the day, so most employees were helping people at the checkout stands and not in the aisles. The clerk, whose name was Billy, was just a kid. He had just started working there, and he apologized for not knowing where the donuts were. This did little to comfort my elevated heart rate, the tightness that formed in my temples and shoulders, and the irritation in my abdominal region.

Returning to the front of the store, I asked one of the cashiers for the location of the donuts. As Murphy's Law would have it, the cashier directed me back again to the back of the store. Apparently, the donuts were on the bottom shelves at the end of aisle four. As I walked yet again to the back, my neck tightened, my pulse rate edged up higher, and I started weighing the decision on which brand of donuts to buy. And, what kind? This was such a stressful dilemma.

I made decisions all day long at work. Yet, was I really stressing over which donuts to purchase? "How ridiculous," I thought. "What the hell...," I audibly murmured. Since my cell phone didn't work in this particular building, and I couldn't ask Eve, I was forced to decide. For a moment, my mind was visualizing the football game starting, and I was probably missing some great play. It seemed that on this day, all of my decisions were bound to be second-guessed by someone anyway. Why should this donut purchase be any different?

I thought the price for the name-brand donuts were way too high. I wondered why anyone would pay so much for sugar and dough. Instead, I chose several boxes of a generic brand, and quickly headed back up to the checkout line.

All of the lines were overflowing with customers and their carts. Looking for the express line, I staked out my place in line. I noticed a lady in front of me who had approximately 25 items in her cart. The sign clearly read "10 Items or less." She shot me a provoking glance. She seemed to know what I was thinking. It was an *ice-cold glare,* or maybe what in some cultures would be called, an *evil eye.* It was as if she was daring me to say something about it. I thought to myself, "Seriously? You are staring me down, so you can be in front of me over donuts? What a day..." I was just too tired to get into any more clashes for the day, and just waited my turn in line.

I did, however, wonder if anyone was observing this lady's indiscretion. I looked around and noticed a supervisor giving instructions to the cashier. It appeared she was just like the clerk I had run into earlier and was also new. The cashier wasn't yet aware of all the store's procedures and was still learning. I recalled something from the news about a grocery store workers' labor strike, which explained why the lines were extra-long. These workers were just trying to do their new jobs and provide for their families. From the body language of the people waiting in line, the fact that these clerks were new wasn't factored into their communications with the newbies.

As I stood in line, going nowhere fast and trying to ignore the lady in front of me, my eyes landed on a magazine cover. Two gorgeous thirty-something movie stars smiled radiantly from the cover. "What perfect lives they must have?" I ruminated. They were super-rich, able to eat at the finest restaurants, travel the world, have adoring fans, and they definitely didn't have to do their own shopping, I hypothesized. I started to fantasize about having their life. For a moment, I even started smiling and felt a little relief in my temples, but then the person behind me suddenly bumped into my back with his cart. To my dismay, the fantasy was abruptly halted... Making things even worse, I had a slight respite from the drudgery with this glimpse of what my life could be like. And now, this fantasy was abruptly taken away nearly as fast as it started.

I knew that my life, by most standards was pretty good. Fantasizing about what my life could have been might leave me even more depressed anyway. I wasn't a rich movie star, and there was no point in pretending that I was; or that having their life was any better than mine. The *evil eye* lady with twenty-five items, had finally paid the cashier, and my purchase was the only smooth event of this scene. I was back in my car and soon to be home.

I again turned my head looking at the ever-patient Christ. He was watching me review the scene at the supermarket. He could see that I was getting it. I was quickly seeing the errors in my interactions with others. He had alluded to a solution to my problems. I was looking forward to the learning of the solutions to my many problems.

Watching the review of my day and this supermarket scene was like eating bad frosting on a mud cake. I had a long list of issues that needed to be overcome. Part of me felt like I was being dragged through the proverbial mud, and this review was only *one* day of my life. Was I like this all the time? Were my emotions this out of control? In a split second, we were back on the *Christ Canopy* watching a new scene.

The Review of Home

Entering our home, I found everything was just as it was when I had left - there was still conflict and chaos. The kids were arguing with each other, and Eve was a bit frazzled. She was more exasperated with the kids than anything else, and this was fatiguing for her. She was, however, grateful that I had picked up the donuts. That gratitude lasted for a brief moment until she opened the bag.

When she saw that I had bought generic donuts and not the fancy name brand, Eve became heated. She probably had bottled up all of any negative emotions from her day. Dealing with her co-workers, her boss, people at the kid's school, and these emotions were like a powder keg ready to explode. "What were you thinking??? What will your son's friends think?" she sternly interrogated. The kids will not be happy over my selection and even worse, our son might get teased. We lived in a pretty nice community, thus everyone was worried about *keeping up with the Joneses.*

Wow! I realized there was sure a lot of pressure in buying just the *right* donuts. Now, I snapped. If I had a pressure regulator in my body, it was now on *burst open* mode and free-flowing. I had put up with a lot of flak from nearly everyone and everywhere my entire day. Now, to take more flack at home, simply because I wouldn't spend an extra $10 to be socially acceptable; was just too much to ask. The argument escalated. Other issues were brought up adding fuel to the already raging fire of animosity. My head felt hot from the drama. My ears were literally red. My neck was stiffening, and my lower back was also tightening. My throat was even beginning to feel soar.

Looking at the Christ after watching this scene, I could swear it made even his all-loving heart ache a little. My heart was sure aching after watching this scene. My actions were deplorable... I made a mental note on just how many physical reactions were happening in my body as a result of this exchange. I did the math. If we fought like this, say every Full Moon, twelve times a year, my body would be put through torture. I remembered back a to memory of about seven years prior when we lived in a town home. I remembered one of my neighbors and I having a conversation that most of the men were out in their garages in around the time of the Full Moon and New Moon, as ironically, they were in a fight with their wives.

Eve and I spent the rest of the evening in icy silence. Not wanting to fight in front of Amy and Allen, we attempted to engage the children in dinner conversation about their day. The children's responses to questions about their day, especially our older child, Allen, were usually monosyllabic responses. Answers like "Good," "Yeah," "No" or "Don't know."

After dinner, I was able to watch a few minutes of the end of the football game and the highlights on the news. I chuckled for a moment that I was watching *highlights* from the game, while I was watching *highlights of my day.* After Eve got the kids in bed, and we were in the privacy of our bedroom, we reinitiated or more accurately, reignited our argument. After a few verbal barks at each other, our tiredness and our love for each other finally quelled the flames of our animated argument. As the tension started dissipating, we apologized to each another. We truly loved each other. Yet even with all that love, arguments still happened and seemingly at a more frequent pace; as our lives became more chaotic. After we both brushed our teeth and did our routine before going to bed, the exhaustion of our day had caught up with us. We were asleep once our heads hit the pillows.

The Christ's lips were always slightly smiling, and his composure was always highly content and peaceful. While his lips, unless he was speaking, hardly moved, I could almost swear he was smiling more after watching this scene, at least that is what I'd like to think.

As I reflected on the reviews, my mind became quite active, as if someone gave me a shot of one of those 5-Hour energy drinks. It was a blur of cognitive function identical to a computer searching for several files at once. I wondered how I could do a better job of keeping my composure with rude drivers, demanding employees, backstabbing co-workers, strangers in the supermarket, and especially not lose it with the people I loved the most - my wife and children. I came to the realization that I lost my temper the most with the one's I loved the most. I thought it was an interesting duality and wished I could come up with an answer to this dilemma. The good news, as it appeared, was that I didn't have to come up with these answers myself, and someone far wiser was going to help me get there!

Waking Up!

Ouch... I was feeling heavy, as I realized I was no longer on the beautiful *Christ Canopy*, and felt the heaviness of being in my physical body. I realized I woke up. It appeared I had fallen asleep in the chair in the CAT Scan waiting room. The left side of my temple hurt, as it hit the pointed top of the most uncomfortable hospital chair in history. I started thinking, "Whoever designed and worse yet purchased these chairs, did so without regard for the people sitting in them."

My inner reflection was interrupted by a tap on my shoulder and a gentle voice, "Mr. O'Connor, Mr. O'Connor, your son can see you now," from the nurse.

Not wanting to startle me, she said I fell asleep for about twenty minutes. She chose not to wake me, as I looked like I needed the rest. She said she had never seen someone smile and frown so many times while they were sleeping; especially for such a short interval of time.

As I was coming into my waking consciousness, I started reflecting and internally asking if I had really had a dream with the Christ. I did, however, feel very different. I was far more refreshed than any power nap I had ever taken. And, despite being in a hospital waiting room, not knowing what was going to happen to our son, I felt like I could cope with any outcome. Better than even being able to deal with the results, I felt like things were going to be okay.

Then it dawned on me. While I had learned a lot about my issues and witnessed many examples of how I needed to improve, I didn't get a chance to learn the **Three Priceless or Precious Techniques** that the Christ alluded to. I couldn't even remember what they were called, and I wondered what I was going to do.

The nurse helped me to my feet, as I was having a little difficulty adjusting to being back in my body, and then guided me to see Allen. Though he should have been scared with all he had been through, Allen was in good spirits. I was very proud of how well he was handling the situation and himself.

The doctor came walking into the room with his head down reviewing Allen's files. In a very detached manner, he said that things appeared stable. Allen would no longer need to stay overnight and was ready to be discharged. The doctor instructed me that we should watch for symptoms like headaches, nausea, sensitivity to light and a few other things. He said that if any of these symptoms arose, to immediately bring him back in. As quickly as he spoke, he left the room, and was off to see another patient. I completed the paperwork and got Allen in the car. Happy to be released from the hospital, Allen and I drove home.

Eve needed to stay home during this ordeal, since she was unable to find someone to watch Amy. The night was supposed to be a festive one, celebrating our anniversary and celebrating Allen's birthday, before it went awry. Eve and Amy lovingly welcomed Allen home with hugs and kisses. We were all physically and emotionally exhausted. Leaving Allen's gifts unopened for the next day, we all went upstairs and went to bed.

We were thankful that Allen was home and most likely going to be OK.

The Three Priceless Techniques Dream

Exhausted from riding the emotional roller coaster of the day, I fell asleep within moments of my head hitting the pillow. It seemed like only minutes when suddenly I heard, "Joe, the life you wished for when you were at the hospital *is possible; it does exist!"* The Christ said, "The world of *Malkuth* that you are living in - is an illusion. It is an illusion of your mind..."

The Christ was sitting on a throne, patiently hovering in the air in this new dream. While his exterior was one of calmness, I could swear he inwardly was excited to share new revelations. Maybe this was just my projection, as I was so relieved and excited that he was back. His radiance showered me with a euphoria of sorts, better than anything I had ever experienced. It was clear to me that I needed to learn something more to cease the misery that I, with my own mind and emotions, was creating for myself and those around me.

While in my dream-state, I was conversing with the Christ, doing reviews of my life and then the illusion of my life began to be clear. It was almost as if everything *was* a dream or rather, as the Christ said, "*Malkuth, an illusion.*" I remembered that before we had reviewed my day, I asked the magic question, "How can I change the illusion?"

The ever-perceptive Christ smiled and said, "Now, I will teach you **Three Priceless Techniques** that will transform your illusion and thus your suffering. Before I teach you the **First Priceless Technique,** what do you see when you look at yourself in the mirror?"

Now in the *Christ Canopy* appeared a full-length mirror on the wall. While I looked at the mirror, I saw a man who was looking tired, losing his hair, losing the virility of his youth, with bags under his eyes, and wrinkles on his forehead. I decided to sum up my existence by answering the Christ with, "I see a *businessman.*"

Again, the Christ didn't change his expression, but from my perspective I thought he kind of simpered. He replied, "**The First Priceless Technique** is that you need to remember *you are a Christ* and that *you have Christ Consciousness within you,*" he specified with such logical tone. "In breaking down the word 'Christian'", he continued, "consists of the words Christ I am." When he spoke, his tone had this most unique quality - there was no demeaning, there were no condescension, there was just resounding truth.

"I am a Christ... What does this mean?" I asked.

The Christ poetically paused for a moment and then said softly with excitement, "It means you have returned and are One with the Divine Father! You are living *outside* this world of physical illusion. A Christ no longer experiences the anguish, misery and suffering that you have experienced in your reviews. A Christ is filled with tranquil abiding, deep peace, empathy and compassion."

He lovingly further explained, "Unfortunately Joe, you are blocking your true *Christ Consciousness,* because you are identifying yourself with *Malkuth* the world of illusion – the physical world that you currently live in and all the thoughts and emotions that go along with it. It is a world of darkness and suffering. If you break down the word enlightenment, it literally means to *lighten the mind.* You see past the Malkuth by removing your heavy, negative emotions and thoughts and replacing them with uplifting emotions like joy and reframing your world to bring in the light that *really* exists."

"But everything exposed by the light becomes visible, for everything that is illuminated becomes a light itself. So, it is said in **Ephesians 5:13-4** 'Wake up, O sleeper, rise up from the dead, and Christ will shine on you.' While it was said, 'the light will shine on you,' it was originally stated as 'shine in you.' In **Luke 11:4-6,** 'The light of the body is the eye: therefore, when thine eye is single, thy whole body also is full of light; but when thine eye is evil, thy body also is full of darkness. Take heed therefore that the light which is in thee be not darkness. If thy whole body therefore be full of light, having no part dark, the whole shall be full of light, as when the bright shining of a candle doth give thee light.' In these passages *Christ Consciousness* is being discussed."

Wow! I thought this conversation was like drinking from a fire hose! For a moment, a doubt popped into my head that I wouldn't be able to understand these teachings, much less deploy them. I didn't even know what lighten the mind meant. While being filled with deep peace sounded great, it also sounded very unrealistic. "How do I change that?" I queried.

"It's really quite simple," answered the Christ. "Close your eyes, put your tongue on the roof of your mouth or palate, and imagine that you are a Glowing Christ. Keep imagining you are a Glowing Christ of pure, bright light, then imagine that a rainbow light is emanating in concentric circles all around you. Continue to imagine these concentric circles of rainbow light growing outward to infinity and see yourself becoming an ever-expanding Glowing Christ."

Whether *my* physical lips were actually moving or not, I couldn't tell. But in the dream, I was grinning from ear-to-ear as I started applying this **Technique**! My body felt lighter and my stress was rapidly dissipating. It was like snow being melted by the warm light and heat from the rays of the Sun. I was in awe to see how fast the **First Priceless Technique** was working. I was experiencing deeper levels of peace with each passing moment. Physically, my shoulders felt like they sunk deep down into the bed. My breathing became deeper yet slower, and my face felt like it was glowing. "Wow*!*" I thought to myself, "This is amazing!*"*

"Joe, the end result of this **Technique** is to bring about your true nature; your *Christ Consciousness.* I will now show you an advanced **Technique** that will help you even more. **Ezekiel 1:4** says, 'And I looked, and, behold, a whirlwind came out of the north, a great cloud, and a fire infolding itself, and a brightness *was* about it, and out of the midst thereof as the color of amber, out of the midst of the fire.' **Ezekiel 1:26** also says, 'Above this surface was something that looked like a throne made of blue lapis lazuli. And on this throne high above was a figure whose appearance resembled a man.' And, **Daniel 7:9** says, 'I beheld till the thrones were cast down, and the Ancient of days did sit, whose garment *was* white as snow, and the hair of his head like the pure wool: his throne *was* *like* the fiery flame, *and* his wheels *as* burning fire.'" Christ sagaciously said.

"Please visualize me descending from the heavens, coming down in *through* the top of your head." The Christ paused for a moment as he watched me comprehend and simulate this initial part of the **Technique**. "As you bring me down through the top of your head and into your body, you merge me into you and you into me. From the center of your heart, you then visualize rainbow concentric circles of light spiraling outward in all directions. The above passages reference fire, which is symbolic for light. Merging with me at the beginning is vital to this **Technique's** success, because it helps bring about the tranquil and empowering energy of the *Christ Consciousness* to help you cultivate your Christhood. The concentric rings of light emerging from your heart help transform the environment around you."

He astutely paused for a moment. My mind was again like a hard drive doing a search query. I realized that by identifying myself as a businessman, I was limiting myself. I knew I was seeing and feeling only the tip of the iceberg of my true existence. To test this new **Technique**, I imagined a new mirror in the *Christ Canopy* and looked at myself as a businessman in the mirror. I could only hold this image for a few seconds. This image was too painful. I started feeling pressure in my head, congestion in my sinuses, and other parts of my body started feeling heavy. "Whew! I said, "Enough of that!"

I changed the image in my *Christ Canopy Mirror* and saw my reflection as a Christ. "Ahhh…" resoundingly went off in my inner ears. I could feel the peace in my mind, body and soul! The Christ was right! Being a Christ was far better than being just a businessman. I let the mirror disappear and turned back to the Christ.

"Once, you've practiced the above **Technique** it will become second nature to you. If you are having challenges to over simplify it, just imagine me coming down and us merging and seeing everything as pure light!" he cogently communicated.

The Christ said it was time for learning **Priceless Technique Number Two.**

"Joe, when you look at your world what do you see?" he asked.

I immediately thought of the review. I saw my tired body wake up in the morning, the conflicts at home, the conflicts on the freeways, the conflict at work and the conflict at the supermarket. I said, "The world is full of conflict! It is a pretty dark place."

The Glowing Christ paused. He gently and sweetly confirmed "You are correct! The world, as you are currently seeing it, from your *Joe perspective* is conflict, sadness, and suffering. While 'yes' there are times of happiness, these times are waning, and suffering is inevitable. As you learn to see the world through your *Christ Consciousness,* you'll move past the world of conform and illusion that is plaguing you and others."

He drew in a breath and his breath and presence seemed to shine even more light into the dream. He said *Malkuth also* means

Kingdom, but it also means Sovereignty. "As we start seeing past our limiting filters through our eyes, feelings, etc., we become Sovereign, and are able to connect to Heaven. To better illustrate, there is a passage in the **Book of Enoch XLI: 1-2** that you may not be familiar with. 'And after that I saw all the secrets of the heavens, and how the kingdom is divided, and how the actions of men are weighed in the balance.' But of course, you also remember, in **Matthew 6:33**, 'But seek ye first the kingdom of God, and his righteousness; and all these things shall be added unto you.'"

He eloquently paused to let this statement sink in. He could see that I remembered this biblical passage and continued.

"Joe, since you are a Christ, you must remember that the *location* you are in, wherever you are, is in a *Christ Castle*. The energy that radiates from your Christ presence inherently can help transform the environment around you into a *Christ Castle*," he clarified. "**Priceless Technique Number Two** is seeing the environment around you and the world in general as a *Christ Castle*. You see past the illusion and see the environment as pure radiant light! In the same way that you saw yourself as a Christ, which was a limited view of yourself, your limited perception is seeing only the darkness in the world. Yes, there is darkness in the world, but you can help transform it." he concluded.

"In **Luke 17:20-21** it is said, 'Now having been questioned by the Pharisees as to when the kingdom of God was coming, He answered them and said, "The kingdom of God is not coming with signs to be observed; nor will they say, 'Look, here it is!' or, 'There it is!' For behold, the kingdom of God is in your midst.' This Kingdom is the *Christ Castle* that I'm referring to. *Christ Castle* is a little catchier, is it not?" he said to me with a wink.

I was so startled by his eloquent grace and now his display of humor. I thought to myself, "Wow, I'm speaking with the Christ in a dream and he is cracking a joke!" We were so serious, and I was learning these deep teachings and maybe he thought I needed a little humor to lighten the mood.

Just learning that I was a Christ was a big mental upgrade. If I was a computer, it felt like I jumped up several levels in my operating system software. It was like I went from DOS to Windows 10. The idea that my being had an effect on my entire environment was the equivalent of moving from a using a floppy disc to a Two Terabyte hard drive.

Inquisitively, I closed my eyes and imagined the world around me transforming into a *Christ Castle*. I visualized the Kingdom of God and its ebullient light illuminating my surroundings. Feeling an even greater level of peace, it now donned on me that peace had levels… My inner chatter slowed. It almost stopped, or rather just silenced.

My inner dialogue was now gone. Well almost gone… my inner dialogue was trying to fight back. It attempted to fill my head once again with chatter and negativity. In an attempt to preserve itself, the dialogue tried to start up again by talking about the lack of talking. It was almost humorous.

Again, I empowered my inner dialogue to subside with greater ease than before. In its place, I experienced stillness and a level of love that I had never encountered before. It was deeper than the love I felt when I held my newborn child for the very first time. The sweetness was sublime. I was in a total state of peace and love, feeling very blissful!

With these profound changes, I was also noticing in my mind and emotions, that there was a corresponding effect on my physical body. As my mind became clearer in thought and quicker in response, my physical eyes felt brighter. The congestion that was normally present in my sinus passages started clearing up, and the underlying tension in my neck and shoulders started loosening. As my newly found sense of *bliss* started increasing, my breathing repetition slowed, and the tension in my chest released. It seemed there was a relationship between this release of tension and the decreasing of my heartbeat. This was a welcome relief for my hypertension, which I suffered from for many years. I could feel my blood pressure slow as my breathing pattern eased.

"Everything in this physical world is an illusion. In ancient Sanskrit they called it Maya and is based on your perception. Photons, for example, are totally invisible until they strike your retina. Sugar is tasteless until it touches your tongue. A rose has no fragrance until your nose inhales the pleasant aroma. The sound of a tree falling doesn't exist until your eardrums make it so. These qualities (technically known as qualia) are produced by the mechanism of perception." To further the point, he added, "Most people would think the color of the Sun is orange or yellow. However, the filter of the earth's energy field and your eyes give it the hue of these colors. When seen from space it is actually a blinding white light!" With the brilliance of the Christ, he eloquently discoursed.

I could mentally see a foreshadowing of a future event; my doctor explaining that I would no longer need my high blood pressure medication. This process was like being in an imaginary spa that worked out the tightness in my body as the serenity of this healing space melted my tension away.

I shared with the Christ that the people in my imaginary Christ Castle were glowing and smiling. I could feel an electrical buzz in the air that was filled with waves of energy. My new level of consciousness seemed to enable me to feel deeper levels of peace, stillness and love. The feelings were similar to those I felt radiating from the Christ, but to a lesser degree.

"Very good, Joe, you are learning quickly," the Christ confidently praised.

"As you've experienced your *Christ Consciousness,* your true nature Joe, it is very easy to imagine that you are a Christ. It is very easy to imagine that all that is around you is a *Christ Castle,* or, in reality the Kingdom of God. Over time, with practice, you will not have to work at this process. It will be easier, and you will be transformed into this natural state," he articulated.

"'But the saints of the Highest One will receive the Kingdom and possess the Kingdom forever, for all ages to come,' **Daniel 7:19** and in the **Gospel of Thomas Verse 3:1-5**, which are not well known say, 'If those who lead you say to you,' and 'Look the Kingdom is in the sky then the birds of the sky will proceed you.' In both of these verses it means that you Joe, must create heaven on earth. You are a co-creator in this process. You need to do this for yourself, to help you with your own suffering and to transform the darkness, war, and the lower natures of man. 'It is in the sea, then the fishes will precede you.' Rather, the Kingdom is inside and outside of you. When you come to know yourself, then you will be known, and you will realize that you are a child of the living Father. But if you do not come to know yourself, then you exist in poverty, and you are poverty." he profoundly stated.

He happily, although his demeanor didn't change as it was just my projection and the reflection of the joy in my heart continued with, "'Thine, O LORD, is the greatness, and the power, and the glory, and the victory, and the majesty: for all that is in the heaven and in the earth is thine; thine is the Kingdom, O LORD, and thou art exalted as head above all' **1 Chronicles 29:11.** This is another great example of our needing to do our job and bring down the Kingdom from above," he said.

He wisely paused to allow me to grasp these verses and continued with, "'Ye are the light of the world. A city that is set on a hill cannot be hid. Neither do men light a candle, and put it under a bushel, but on a candlestick; Let your light so shine before men, that they may see your good works, and glorify your Father which is in heaven, and it giveth light unto all that are in the house' **Matthew 5:14-16.** This passage refers to you are glorifying God by letting your light shine and creating the Kingdom of God on earth!" he shared.

"One of my favorite versus is also from the **Gospel of Thomas 113:1-4,** 'His disciples said to him: The kingdom — on what day will it come? It will not come by watching (and waiting for) it. They will not say: 'Look, here!' or 'Look, there! Rather, the Kingdom of the Father is spread out upon the earth, and people do not see it.' Joe, when a racecar driver is racing at a high-speed, he never looks at the rail. He keeps his focus ahead of him. Keep your eyes on the Kingdom and see it everywhere!" he proclaimed.

"Just to recap Joe, your job is to seek the Kingdom of God, which is the higher form of *Malkuth,* and by helping to build the Kingdom of God on earth, you become *Sovereign.* 'Then Huram continued, "Blessed be the LORD, the God of Israel, who has made heaven and earth, who has given King David a wise son, endowed with discretion and understanding, who will build a house for the LORD and a royal palace for himself.' **2 Chronicles 2:22,** 'If you do not abstain from the world (the illusion) you will not find his Kingdom' **Gospel of Thomas 27:1,"** he shared.

I was overjoyed at hearing about these scriptures and now understanding them at an entirely new level.

Similar to how I tested the concepts learned with **Priceless Techniques Number One**, I imagined looking at the world from my normal *Joe perspective.* Talk about a crash landing... I literally felt like I was dropped from the heavens when I looked at the world through these *Malkuth goggles.* The world looked even darker than before, the people that I worked with looked a little *ghoulish.*

I quickly reverted my vision back to my *Christ Vision.* Instead of seeing just the conflicts and alike, I now saw people as

Souls. I got a glimpse on how these conflicts darkened their Souls with hideous energies around them. It was a little scary... But, I now understood why people were literally chained to suffering without this *Christ Vision.*

The Christ observed that I was getting a little scared at this new realization. Seeing the true nature of others was a little shocking, but I think he knew that I could handle it. It was probably best that I realized that I was on this path of being tethered to *Malkuth and* seeing this new reality would provide extra motivation to get out of it!

The Christ poetically paused and asked, "Are you ready for **Priceless Technique Number Three?**"

I got the feeling by the way he said it that this **Technique** was going to be harder. The first two were pretty easy, so there must be some sort of catch with the third. Maybe I had to put myself into some yogic pretzel for 24 hours, wander in the desert for 40 days, fly off to the Himalayas, give away all my worldly possessions or walk around in a robe and grow a beard. These were the visuals that popped into my head. I wondered what it could be. With inner exuberance and a slight apprehension, I answered, "Yes!"

"As I said," the Christ continued, "The first two **Techniques** are very easy to apply. The **Third** is also easy; however, most people will find it difficult to apply at first. With practice, this **Technique** will be the most rewarding for you, and it will help others as well!"

"Joe, imagine seeing someone that you love," Christ said. I immediately imagined my daughter, Amy. "She is so sweet and adorable," I thought to myself. The Christ could see me smiling. "Joe," he countered "Imagine someone you don't like." I imagined one of my co-workers and in mind's eye, she looked like a witch. In fact, I imagined hearing her fake laugh, sounding like a witch's, chilling laugh."

I started hearing her say "My pretty…" and the Christ wisely interrupted with "What is the difference in how you *see* these people?"

I had never really thought about it. The way I saw others just popped into my head and just seemed normal to judge others. I thought for a moment and replied, "When I see Amy, I'm focused on her good qualities while my co-worker's negative qualities stick out like a sore thumb."

The Christ started a new declaration, "As you learned in the **First Two Priceless Techniques,** the world you are living in is an illusion, like a dream, a world of your ordinary perceptions. The physical world is an illusion, and the real world is the Kingdom of God, where everything is pure light. The Essenes knew that everything is light. It is interesting that science is still trying to teach that there is a speed of light, when everything *is* light. Most people, when read the Bible miss the clue in **Numbers 2:9** where it says, 'All the men assigned to the camp of Judah, according to their divisions, number 186,400. They will set out first.' In science, light is said to travel at approximately 186,000 miles per second. The symbolism here is the Tribe of Judea were actually

Children of Light. You now have a greater understanding of that reality, from when you yourself turned into a Christ and saw the world as a *Christ Castle* and now you also see everything as light!"

"When you were annoyed with drivers on the freeway, irritated with your boss, maddened by your co-workers, aggravated with people in the grocery store, and upset with your children and your wife; all of these thoughts and emotions were emanating from your *non-Christ Consciousness nature.* You were seeing darkness... To make matters worse, the negative perceptions you held towards these people projected negative energies at them. These negative energies affected *their internal organs, their energetic Castle* and further diminished *their Christ within.* Along with this damage towards them, there was a rebound effect as it damaged you as well."

"So," maintained the Christ, "Since you are a Christ, having *Christ Consciousness,* you would never harm anyone or anything. By applying this principle, you certainly wouldn't hurt anyone physically, nor would you hurt anyone with your mind (your thoughts) or your speech."

He paused for a moment to let this sink in. The depth of his words touched my heart and touched the depths of my soul. The Christ was right. I had never thought about harming others with thought.

"'Thou shall not kill' is a Commandment that you hear all the time, but it has been mistranslated... In Aramaic it was 'Thou shall not steal someone's spirit...' In other words, your words could harm someone even more than a physical altercation. In fact, suicide is so prevalent today because someone's spirit is crushed by a mean Tweet or a Facebook posting," he revealed.

"Each person, whether you choose to like them or not, is only human... just like you. They are just people while here on Earth, on their way to reaching their Christ Nature. Some are farther down the path than others. Many have just started. By using **Priceless Technique Number Three,** you must remember that others are Christs too, and to see them as Christs!" he finished.

For the first time in my dreams with the Christ, I was a little disenchanted. I felt some trepidation as to whether I could actually apply this last precious pearl of wisdom that the Christ had so freely given me. Just like when I was fantasizing in line at the supermarket of having a life that movie stars led, my fantasy easily slipped away when a cart hit me in the back. I could feel my consciousness and energy contracting with the return of my inner dialogue.

He went on to impart, "'But I say unto you which hear, Love your enemies, do good to them which hate you, Bless them that curse you, and pray for them which despitefully use you,' **Luke 6:27-28** and **Luke 6:35** says, 'But love ye your enemies, and do good, and lend, hoping for nothing again; and your reward shall be great, and ye shall be the Children of the Highest: for he is kind unto the unthankful and to the evil, '"

From my now jaded perspective, I believe the Christ tried to give me reassurance by sharing more scriptures to inspire me. I just realized the word "inspire" means "in spirit" and he was trying to infuse me with spirit. I now realized that Children of the Highest were Children of Light or Sons of God! WOW!!! My mind was blown. I could have sworn the Christ gave me an even bigger smile, as he saw my consciousness was expanding and becoming more Christ-like. I could have sworn he said, "There will be more on this later!"

With profound wisdom and compassion, the Christ suggested that I simply give it a try. He said, "Imagine yourself at the office in a sales meeting, and see your boss complimenting you for exceeding your sales quota, then taking it away by saying you needed to do more in the next quarter."

The Christ's smile and the simplicity of his words put me at ease. His radiance was something to behold. I reflected that, under these circumstances, my co-workers would have feelings of jealousy. They would only hear the compliment part, and conveniently ignore the next quarter part of the communication. Also, while they might not outwardly show it, they would unconsciously be glaring at me with the energy of envy. Now I was able to feel this *envy energy* even in the dream. The Christ stated that the world of light (energy) was more *real* than the physical realm. Recalling these words, it became clear I was full of understanding.

I loved being on the *Christ Canopy* as it brought out my *Christ Intelligence,* too. I was able to easily put concepts together. I reflected on expressions that we used daily and how the colors used in these idioms reflected energy. "Green with envy," meant jealousy. "Feeling blue today," denoted sadness. "A yellow-belly," reflected someone who was afraid. "My ears are burning (red)…" demonstrated how dirty, red emotional energy was being directed at others. "Whoa! I loved these realizations!" I concluded.

It now donned on me that as a Christ, I would also have access to omniscience, as well. I could swear the Christ did one of those *smiles at yet another realization* and said, "Let's continue…"

The Christ told me to once again to imagine myself becoming a Christ of pure light with rainbow light emanating, and then to see the boardroom and the building as a *Christ Castle*. The Christ stated to re-imagine my boss and co-workers turning into Christs of pure light by applying **Priceless Technique Number Three.** With apprehension, I followed the steps, and much to my amazement; I felt an incredible sense of lightness and relief. A feeling of bliss took me even higher than I had felt earlier in the dream. "Wow, the Christ was right!" I gleefully said in my head. "This **Priceless Technique** was the crown jewel of the **Three!!!**

He further added, that if at any time I was in a rush, or having challenges imagining rainbow light, that I could substitute pure light. And, see everything as pure light!

I couldn't remember if a biblical quote was or not, but I remembered always hearing 'Find God in all things,' or in other words 'Find God in others.' This now meant something new and revealing to me.

In this moment of reflection, I realized a profound similarity. The similarity of being and seeing people as pure light. I remembered that the word *enlightenment* meant making the mind light, and not entangled with gray, dirty, heavier energy. "Light felt good," I thought.

"To recap Joe, when you see others through the filter of your heart and your *Christ Consciousness* you are fulfilling the mission stated in **2 Corinthians 4:6** 'For God, who commanded the light to shine out of darkness, hath shined in our hearts, to give the light of the knowledge of the glory of God in the face of the Christ.'"

My lips seemingly moved on their own accord as I started smiling. I never realized until now just how much stress I had previously carried in my facial muscles, let alone the rest of my body. It felt like I was *being lifted and feeling weightless*. It was much easier to want to stay in this state.

"How many people know about these **Three Priceless Techniques?**" I asked.

"Not enough," wittily replied the Christ.

"Who would have thought that the Christ, along with his omniscience, also possessed humor, timing and wit?" I quixotically thought. Realizing it might have only been my imagination, I could also feel a sense of sadness emanating from the Christ. Actually, more like compassion. I could feel him wanting others to know of these **Techniques**. I also saw in his body language, that he wanted people to stop ignorantly hurting each other with their words, thoughts and interactions. This realization gave me a boost of energy - a confidence and a purpose. I felt like I was part of something bigger than myself.

"Well," I said, "how many people would be enough?"

"Great question!" the Christ fired back. "There are approximately seven billion people on the physical world on earth. If seven million or more would apply the **Three Priceless Techniques**, it would create a wave of energy, literally a positive tsunami of energy. If done simultaneously and consistently, it could transform the physical world into a *Christ Castle... forever.*"

The Christ further explained when a person becomes a Christ, their energy field (Castle) expands more than ten times. As they create a *Christ Castle*, the frequency of that location is also purified and multiplied by yet another ten plus times. And, as other people do it together at the same location, the energy is multiplied by still another ten-fold. He alluded to speaking more about the group application of these **Priceless Techniques** at another time and how it dramatically multiplied everything.

"So, you see Joe, the Earth needs at least seven million people doing these **Techniques** simultaneously," the Christ concluded.

I mentally did the math. 7,000,000 people multiplying their energy 10 times, the energy of the location 10 times and simultaneously multiplying the energy of others by 10; that might just equal seven hundred million people, or roughly 1/10th of 1% of the population. The wave of *Christ Castle*s from this number of people could be enough to help all seven billion people. The Christ seemed to be smiling even more, so I was on to something. I thought it was pretty cool I could do math in a dream!

A New Day

Boom! I landed in my body... Crash landing back into the physical world felt very heavy. The alarm was screeching... While it was still an annoying sound, in my head, I transformed the claxon sound to play U2's *A Beautiful Day*. The Christ dream was gone, however, the remnants of what he taught me remained. It was now time for the reality and heaviness of the physical world. As the weight of my hand hit the alarm clock, it seemed a bit *lighter*.

I collected myself as I showered. My negative internal dialogue started... I now dubbed this dialogue o*ld Joe Talk* who tried to deny the dream's existence. My newfound countenance quickly shrugged this dialogue off. It also seemed as if the world of dreams and the *real* world were merging... With the highest mental and emotional clarity that I had ever experienced, I recounted the **Three Priceless Techniques,** *"Become a Christ, check! Transform the surrounding area into a Christ Castle (the Kingdom of God or, pure light), check! And, most importantly, visualize everyone in that Christ Castle as a Christ of pure light emanating around them, check!"*

In the shower, I imagined myself as a Christ. I felt the anticipated stress of the day begin to melt away, just like it had happened in the dream. I could feel my sinuses clearing, my shoulders relaxing, and my blood pressure dropping. These physical responses were confirmation that the **Techniques** were working.

I then imagined the house, in all its hustle and bustle, as a *Christ Castle* and my lovely wife and children as Christs. I chuckled as I saw Eve and the kids as Christs. It was very easy to do, since I loved them so much.

I saw my son Allen smiling, recalling his state of mind just a few nights before. I realized the experience of being in the hospital was over and felt more like a distant memory. It was amazing knowing that while the concussion experience did occur, my emotions, attachments and suffering were transformed after the review. For lack of a better explanation, the experience was like a *bad dream* and now only a distant, fleeting memory.

As we each prepared for the day and ate breakfast, there seemed to be a rhythm to the house. The energy of the house seemed to slow down quite a bit – as if the house was relaxed, too. Each task was accomplished with greater ease and efficiency. It seemed as if Eve, Allen and Amy each had a slight smile on each of their faces. I, in particular, had a smile on my face watching this new, surreal *real* world happen before my eyes.

Kissing Eve while leaving out the front door was magical! When our lips met, it felt like our energy Castles merged, as if to create an electrical spark! The positive energy of the house seemed to also affect our physical chemistry. I didn't want to leave her caress and looked forward to more of this sensation when I got home.

As I drove down the familiar 404 highway, I visualized the bumper-to-bumper traffic as a *Christ Castle* of multi-colored, metallic chariots each carrying Christs. I really liked this creative visualization and thought the Christ would be proud of my improvisation. Within a few minutes of driving, two drivers cut me off. After encountering two of these *asphalt battles*, I normally would have been yelling at them, or even worse. Instead, I mentally blessed them with greater awareness and consideration towards their fellow drivers. Each time I did this, I noticed my demeanor become serene. As if by magic, the cutting off stopped. Normally each negative event would worsen my mood, escalate my negative emotions and elevate my blood pressure. Now, each negative experience was transformed into a positive one. These **Techniques** were truly transformative, as each interaction made me feel even better! The rest of the drive flowed with ease. I arrived in the office parking lot at what seemed to be a record-breaking time of 30 minutes. Instead of feeling drained, I felt invigorated!

Sally, the receptionist, was engaged in multiple conversations and looked stressed. I immediately saw the office as a *Christ Castle*, and saw her transforming into a Christ of luminous light. I imagined the rainbow light that she was radiating going through the phone. As I walked past her, I thought I could feel her rainbow Castle of energy changing. If I wasn't mistaken, it appeared to grow larger and gently merge through mine. Our collective energies were merging, and we were transforming the environment together. This interaction planted seeds within my consciousness for later exploration.

Grasping the handle of my office door, I heard her tone change and could hear that she was surely smiling as she warmly greeted new callers and effortlessly helped re-connect those on hold. "So far so good," I thought. "This was easy!"

The Company Meeting

Placing my briefcase on the desk, I pulled out my iPad and clicked on the calendar app. At the top of my daily calendar viewed *8 AM, Sales Meeting* in Conference Room A.

While peering out the office window to take in the spectacular site below, I checked my watch. "It was 7:53 AM, just enough time to visit the men's room and walk upstairs to the meeting,"

As I walked into the conference room, my royal *Christ Garb* was starting to fray and come apart at the seams. My *old Joe Talk* reared its ugly head. It tried to pull my mood down by suggesting how long and boring this meeting would be. I imagined the voice moving farther and farther away from me, and soon disappeared. As the negative talk was moving further away in my consciousness, it felt like Angels were like little seamstresses repairing my *Christ Garb*.

By 8:20 the usual routine had occurred; consisting of a review of the prior week, projections for the current week, and I was both praised and pressured by my boss. The praise lacked sincerity - feeling more like lip service. The pressure was always there. My weekly goals were the highest of the team, as there were always high-expectations of my results.

My boss Jackson was more concerned about his own success, though. While some managers like to empower leaders, his style was to create followers. I watched many times how, instead of empowering people and supporting them; he just took their territories away and made excuses to justify it.

The more I succeeded, the more he wanted to remind me who was the boss. However, when I underperformed, the blame fell on me... He was always quick to remind us that his boss, Mr. Stuebe chose him for the job to manage all of us.

The toughest part of these meetings wasn't how Jackson made me feel, but the palpable envy from my co-workers and from Jennifer Cassidy, in particular. As much as I tried to ignore her, the fact was that Jennifer was a fiery and power-hungry salesperson. She wanted to take my position within the company. In fact, she wanted it so badly she maximized every opportunity to create a division between Jackson and myself. She had a master plan... She had her sights on Jackson's boss, the CEO and President, Charles Stuebe and was vying to be his *Hand of the King*. Jennifer even resorted to power plays and innuendos, which had really damaged my reputation in the company for the past eighteen months.

Sitting in the conference room, I thought to myself, "Seeing my family as Christs and seeing other driver's as Christs, was easy. But how could I possibly see Jennifer as a Christ? It would have been easier to view her as a devil than a Christ..."

The meeting dragged on, as these meetings tended to do, with each person adding lengthy and poorly communicated mini-filibusters. In spite of the boredom I was experiencing, I was having no problem seeing myself as a Christ. As I mentally recalled past meetings with Jackson and Jennifer, my *Christ Garb* started fading. With this inner struggle, I had to work harder to re-amplify my Christ splendor. The visual of the conference room as a Christ Castle, and my co-workers as Christ's emanating rainbow light was a struggle to hold in my mind. These steps were being pretty well executed until jealousy started filling the room. Jennifer was torching me with her *mental flamethrower.* My emotional and mental state dropped instantly... My finely tailored *Christ Garb* was now developing holes and looked like it was purchased at a second-hand Halloween shop.

I tried to laugh it off by imagining the fire was only singeing my garb, and not burning it; but, to no avail...

I could no longer feel the smooth buzz of the imagined Christ Castle, as the light was vastly diminishing. I could now feel prickly, hot energy coming at me, slung effusively and carelessly by Jennifer.

I started feeling like the *old Joe*, my old self; pre-anything Christ related Joe... Instead of feeling empowered and *Christ-like*, I felt very disappointed with myself. I started even feeling less than the *old Joe,* because I thought I should have been better at applying these **Techniques.** I had moved so far forward, at least so I thought. Now, I had regressed backwards even further... My sinuses were acting up. I again had tension in my head, neck and back. I also felt like I needed to take my hypertension medication. I really felt like a failure.

I came to the conclusion that if I was observant, my body would tell me what I needed to work on. I pondered, "Awareness is a powerful thing!"

Before the dream, I was more somber than depressed. Having felt bliss and peace, I now knew what being depressed felt like, as I was now experiencing it. Now more than anything, I wanted inner peace! This vacillation of my emotions, and thus suffering, was maddening.

My breathing raced uncontrollably; my thoughts soared around like vultures in my headspace. I replayed the Christ dream over and over again in my head, but I wasn't able to come up with a solution as to how to handle this particular situation.

The Three Priceless Techniques were truly priceless, and now appeared as if they were no longer afforded to me. My inner dialogue went to a negative place. My o*ld Joe Talk* was cutting my *Christ Garb* to shreds. I was now doubting that I could have success applying the **Techniques**. "Sure, these **Techniques** worked in dreams, but this was real life after all," I justified.

After the meeting, I went back to my office and closed the door. I recomposed myself by doing the visualizations. I sought to bring myself out of this *old Joe*-style funk, by applying the **Three Priceless Techniques**. After a few minutes, I still wasn't feeling 100% *Christ-like*, but concluded I was maybe at 72%. From the depths of disappointment, to being somewhat *Christ-like*, was a remarkable achievement in my eyes. I reflected on the gamut of emotions that I was experiencing on a daily basis. I resolved that I wanted to maintain this *tranquil abiding* state of being that the Christ wisely referenced. It was at this moment, I made the mental resolution to end this emotional roller-coaster!

I had to drop off some forecasts to Cheryl, Jackson's secretary. She always treated me dispassionately. She was young, lacked education, and had no real business experience prior to Jackson hiring her. Jackson valued her devotion and loyalty to him and him alone. "Maybe it was because he hired Cheryl without any experience that she reciprocated loyalty outside of work?" I mused. She usually spoke with employees on Jackson's behalf, in a demeaning manner, which typically left them with a bad taste in their mouth. We weren't very motivated by Jackson as a whole, or as she reminded us to call him, "Mr. Jones."

Little did Jackson realize that his choice in an assistant cost him production, as her coldness demotivated us even more. This judgement dropped me further down on the *Christ scale to* maybe 34% as I know these thoughts were not *Christ-like*.

The Christ said it would take consistency, work, diligence and time. I hoped it wouldn't take too long for me to act *Christ-like* on a regular basis. My *Christ Garb* was regaining form as my inner dialogue started thinking positively, "Thirty-four percent Christ-like was certainly better than 100% *old Joe-like*." The awareness of my self-talk was really coming to the forefront of my consciousness. And, more importantly, I was able to distinguish which voice was winning; *old Joe* vs. *Christ-like Joe.*

The drive home was better. The transition from work to my home was exceeding my hopes. I again visualized the cars as metallic chariots carrying their Christs safely home. This visualization always made me chuckle, and I hoped the Christ would be proud of my improvisation of **Techniques Two and Three.** I was much more relaxed, and I smiled a few times; even when a few cars cut me off. I made it home about seven minutes quicker than normal.

The interactions at home were also better. In fact, they were incredible! The connectedness amongst my family was at an all-time high! I felt like I was not only becoming more sensitive to my own energy Castle, but to the energy Castles of those around me. It felt as if our collective energy Castles melted into one. Eve, Allen, Amy and I seemed to merge our rainbow energy into one large, powerful Castle. The Christ briefly mentioned that he'd speak with me at a later date about the power of groups. I was really looking forward to that conversation.

The ability to sense this energetic connection with others was very precious. I mentally flashed back to my family's chaotic interaction from yesterday and was happy that these same three people were glowing so brightly. My positive feelings for them were also magnified. It was pretty cool making our home into a *Christ Castle* with four powerful Christ's radiating rainbow lights concentrically to infinity!

Once my body was lying in bed and my head hit the pillow, I reviewed my day and was quite pleased with the positive developments. I was happy with myself that I had overcome this bump in the road. Everything was just as the Christ had explained, mostly ups with some downs. Overall, I was prevailing in elevating my consciousness, and willingly sharing the *Christ Castle energies* with those around me. Yes, there were some downs to overcome, but I was confident that I would prevail. I had never had so much optimism in my life. I felt this to be my new reality. With an even lighter heart and state of being, I drifted off into a deep slumber.

As I slept, my consciousness was taken back to the *Christ Canopy.* The Christ complimented me on a job well done. This time I was even more aware of the Christ's presence, and seemed to be even more receptive to his teachings. "More alert, if that was possible in this dream?" I laughed inwardly. I somewhat reluctantly and ashamedly asked the Christ, "How could I do better with **Priceless Technique Number Three,** particularly with someone whom I was not altogether very fond of, like Jennifer?"

I laughed at the words coming out of my mouth in this dream "not altogether fond of…" The Christ knew I would have normally said, "a witch like Jennifer." While he again didn't change his demeanor, nor his facial expression, I could swear my new verbiage made him chuckle, too.

The Christ, with a firm but compassionate tone, said, "Joe, being on an emotional roller coaster is *un-Christ like*. It is a human tendency that you must endeavor to transcend. Highs and lows, emotionally and mentally, are only based on perceptions of the physical world - a transitory world," he said.

"Remember Joe," the Christ continued, "The 'tranquil abiding' part of the teachings? You need to maintain a sense of peace and tranquility always, no matter what is happening."

This time, I gratefully grasped this concept on a much deeper level.

"Precious Joe, let me give you a few more methods to accomplish **Priceless Technique Number Three.** These will make it easier for you to deal with people in your life such as Jennifer," he proclaimed.

"The normal method is to visualize the person in the form of a Christ, as you have done." He further clarified by saying, "Except this time, do not see them as a person in their physical body, but rather dissolve their form into formless white light, like a ball of energy with consciousness. This will help you to detach from your perception of their human qualities. Remember how you felt tonight when you and your family melted together into one energy Castle?" he queried.

He paused for a moment seeing whether I grasped this concept. Seeing that I had, he proceeded. "This **Technique** will be easier to use on people like Jennifer because you can depersonalize your *Malkuth,* the physical world perceptions of people and realize that we are all one. Physically, yes, we are separate, but spiritually we are all one." He eloquently proclaimed.

His profoundness comforted me.

"Additionally, let me give you another method that will help you get to **Priceless Technique Three** with greater ease," the Christ went on. "To help you develop more compassion for others, you can visualize any person as your own mother," the Christ explained.

"My mother???" I interrupted.

I just realized that in this dream state with the Christ, thinking thoughts and speaking were the same thing. In previous dreams, we sometimes communicated without our lips moving. I made a mental note to discuss this communication concept more with the Christ at a later juncture.

"Yes, your mother!" replied the Christ. The Christ further answered, reading my mind. "Your mother experienced great pain in delivering you. She fed you. She changed your diapers and kept you safe. She also made many sacrifices for your betterment. A mother loves her child more than she loves herself. If you visualize every person as your mother and treat them with the same level of love and respect; in time it will help you overcome your previous negative tendencies and projections towards that person," He shared.

After his poetic pause, he went on to say, "When you've interacted in the past with Jackson's assistant Cheryl, you were concentrating on the feeling of her being cold to you. Concentrating on this coldness diminishes the loving energy in your heart and in her heart. While, yes, it would be most ideal if Jennifer was easier to work with, this is not to be expected by everyone. There are four main energetic compositions that each person has inherently created, and hers is more inward. We will cover these four compositions more in the future."

With regards to Jennifer, "You are correct in that she has negative intent towards you, and we'll work on that later; however, you have more work to do on yourself. Meanwhile, she is still young, and you need to tap into the creative powers of your *Christ Consciousness*, and see her growing into a more effervescent being," explained the Christ.

I pondered, "Wow, I'm learning a lot here, but there is still more to go!"

"I will give you yet another method, Joe, because in time you will be sharing these **Three Priceless Techniques** with others, and you will need different strategies for different people. For people with *pride* as their stumbling block, you can rapidly diminish this emotion by visualizing others as a Christ and prostrating at their feet."

"Prostrate?!" blurted out of my mouth, while I was thinking, *you have got to be kidding me...* I exclaimed, "How can you prostrate in front of someone you don't like or respect?"

The Christ responded patiently, "Would you prefer working off your pride in this relationship by mentally doing prostrations which will eventually overcome your own pride? Or... would you rather maybe, lose your own prostate?" I thought I heard the Christ making a dirty joke to emphasize the correlation. Or, maybe that was just my dirty imagination. I was beginning to understand the Christ on a higher level. I felt as if some of my bad habits, or in this case, my bad humor, was coming up and being cleared.

The Christ paused allowing me a few minutes to reflect. When he continued he said, "When pride is a major stumbling block, life will knock you to your knees... Pride will cause you to have relationship challenges, financial challenges, and health challenges. Pride will drop you to your knees, but it is up to you how you get there... You can do physical prostrations and mental prostrations to negate this pride, or you can choose *real-life* painful scenarios like losing your prostrate that will kneel you to the floor. The choice is up to you, Joe."

It was the first time the Christ had been so lovingly direct with me. I reflected that, when presented this way, the Christ's teaching along with his demeanor, had a fatherly aspect to it. It moved me. It nudged me out of my own ego, and into the realization that this **Technique** might work. And...I really needed to make it work. I realized that I still had my pride to work on. Imagining myself prostrating to a person full of pride would be challenging to my ego at first, but I believed that it would be very, very effective.

I judged Jackson as having a lot of pride, so I took control of the dream. The *Christ Canopy* was like a laboratory for testing theories. I came to realize it was there for my sole betterment. I chuckled, "The word *sole in sole betterment* was ironic, as it was surely *soul betterment.*" "I loved the realizations I made from my time with the Christ," I humbly thought.

I continued with testing the concept of prostrations. "Since, we are all one," I thought, "If Jackson has pride, then I must have pride, too!" I could feel my *Christ Garb* looking particularly regal. I started at first with a bow, like is commonly practiced in Japan. I felt the area around my heart and the top of my head expand. "So far so good," I mentally said.

Maybe, it was my *pride,* but I felt like I had to transform Jackson into a bigger Christ to prostrate in his general direction. My *Christ Garb* now felt like it needed dry cleaning, as I was clearly judging Jackson, again. In my mind, I completely transformed Jackson into a huge Christ. I initiated the prostrating at Jackson's *Christ* feet. After about the third, mental prostration, I felt my Christ Garb becoming cleaner and I started to feel like I was an even larger Christ. "Hmm…" I considered, "Maybe, whatever I see myself prostrating towards, I become?"

I perceived Jackson's biggest issue as pride. I pondered about Jennifer for a moment. I viewed her as far eviller. At this moment, I didn't honestly feel ready to prostrate towards her. The Christ watched me and said, "Joe, a diamond has many facets. Truth has many levels. It is good that you help her reach her potential as a Christ. As you develop further, we'll work on more **Techniques** for someone who has evil intent and how to minimize it."

He continued, "Lastly, Joe, there is a simple **Technique** that can be done anywhere at any time. It is particularly great in a business situation, where you do not have a lot of time, and you find yourself losing your cool. You can mentally visualize the other person as a Christ and say 'The Christ within me salutes the Christ within you.' This method will help melt away the mental, emotional and obscurations that you have for the other person, and that they have for you. The more challenged the relationship, the more you need to repeat this **Technique**. Your connections with others travel through different levels, but let's save that yet, for another time."

The Next Sales Meeting

At the next weekly sales meeting, I put the **Techniques** to the test. I felt like I was at the spiritual gym, and this time I was going to cover the heavy weights section. Heavy weights have greater resistance, and thus build bigger muscles, or in this case, more developed spiritual muscles.

Mentally, I remade myself into a Christ seeing the room as a *Christ Castle*. I visualized everyone in the room as a Christ emitting rainbow light, especially Jennifer. I made a major transformation in the way I saw her. I was now grateful for her. Rather than seeing her as an impediment or opponent, I now saw her as an instrument to my personal growth - as a teacher. I concentrated on her being the brightest and lightest Christ in the room. Like the improvisation of the metallic chariots, I felt pretty good about this one, as well. As I visualized her as a bigger Christ, I too felt myself becoming an even bigger Christ!

My sales results for the previous week were the best I ever had! Was this a mere coincidence? My attitude and assured ease seemed to create a magnetic affect in my business life. I thought because of my sales results and recognition, Jennifer would be ready with her *evil eye*. As Jackson read off the numbers and complimented me on my outstanding results, something unusual happened. Jennifer was actually smiling and seemed genuinely happy for me. In fact, she congratulated me after the meeting. I remembered the Christ's warning not to get too emotionally high or low over circumstances. Although I don't actually remember when he taught me this, I just knew the Christ affirmed this. So, instead of allowing myself to get too excited, or take credit for the change in Jennifer, I just went inside and felt deep gratitude for my new way of living life. The warmth that was in my heart was indescribable. It was electrifying and quite possibly the most effervescent feeling I had ever experienced.

The rest of the day consisted of different interactions resulting in successfully manifesting *Christ Castles.*

Dream Time

That night as I drifted off to sleep, I was looking forward to being with the Christ and reviewing my day.

The Christ sure enough appeared as he had in our previous encounters. He said, "There is much, much more to learn. At this time in your evolvement, before receiving more, you are to work on and gain even more proficiency in these **Three Priceless Techniques.**"

I was evolving, but this required time, process and even mistakes. He said, "There are only two mistakes one can make along the road to truth. Not going all the way and not starting."

I realized I needed time to perfect them. I told him, "I was committed to going all the way!" For a brief moment I felt like he was leaving me, but I quickly realized that he would never do that. He had given me so much, and I needed to repay his kindness by applying these **Three Priceless Techniques.** And, with that, I could swear he gave me one of those smiles of approval and was gone…

The Christ Castles Challenge

Thank you for reading *Christ Castles!* I hope you enjoyed the story and the experience!

Are you up for a challenge? While you might have trepidation about applying **The Three Priceless Techniques** as to whether they will work for you; I challenge you to take the **Christ Castles Challenge!**

It is said that it takes twenty-one days to create a habit. The **Christ Castles Challenge** is a commitment to practice **The Three Priceless Techniques** for the next twenty-one days. Put them to the test and see how you feel and how much you've progressed on your own *Christ-Scale*. Your world will be much improved!

It is also a good idea to read this book, at least once a week each during this time, as you'll most assuredly understand more and experience more.

As you read, the goal is to inspire seven million people to do **The Three Priceless Techniques** consistently. Please let us know that you are committed to this challenge and email us at ChristCastlesChallenge@gmail.com. We are here to support you in creating your own global Christ Castles Groups.

To further help you to improve your world and the world at large, we highly recommend you do the ***Christ Castles Blessing Meditation*** daily. This twenty-two-minute meditation will accelerate your Christ Nature and help the world to do the same.

You will soon be able to download it at www.ChristsCastle.com for only $9.

As self-published author, you can make a major difference. Reviews are priceless! Sharing is caring. If you deemed this book valuable, please share your thoughts in an *Amazon* review.

Again, thank you for reading this book. I believe that a picture is worth a thousand words, and an experience is worth a million. While you may want to *tell* others about what you learned, it is better that you *recommend* the book to others; so they may have their own *experience*.

I hope to meet you soon in a Christ Castle!

Love,

Daniel O'Hara

Dedication

I would like to dedicate *Christ's Castle* to my beloved Teacher, Choa Kok Sui. He is as close to a Christ in the physical form as I have had the pleasure of knowing. His twenty-two plus years of guidance, blessings, and teachings have given my heart so much joy. He has blessed my family with abundance, has given me the ability to heal others, and given me wisdom to share his teachings, improving the lives of others.

One night in February of 2004, I was lying in bed and asking for guidance on a business transaction, and in a split-second, I was flooded with images of this book. This experience was undeniable, and many of the ideas and events in this book were not in my consciousness until this experience. Who would have thought that during Super Bowl #38 when the Patriots beat the Panthers, I would have translated these images into this story?

Acknowledgments

I would like to thank my lovely ex-wife Eden, who in many ways is more of a Christ than I am. Her years of patience with my growth, support, as well as her stunning, overflowing compassion for others, is awe-inspiring. Our children, A.J. and Alexis, who from the moment they were born, opened my heart to new levels. These three beautiful Christs have helped me a great deal in the creation of this book.

I would like to thank my parents Pat and Lou O'Hara. While they might never acknowledge the existence of their Christhood in this life, they will make great Christs in the future. My father transitioned on his 85th birthday and my greatest regret in life is not having the wisdom to apply these **Techniques** in my younger years with him.

I would like to thank my Aunt Emma, who showered me with unconditional love and was an incredible example of giving of oneself to others. I wish I could have understood her desire to give to others so selflessly when I was younger. She funded most of my training with my Teacher, Choa Kok Sui, and without her, this journey of helping others might never have occurred. In fact, I had a most compelling dream with her while on a retreat with my Teacher. She appeared to me with the most amazing confirmation of her benefitting from my training.

I have always tried to forget any bad events or financial woes in my life. However, during those times of strife, there is a short list of people who exceeded the bar in helping me and my family.

One thing that is constant in this physical life is change. We have upward cycles and downward cycles, and the people who help you during those challenging times are to be honored and cherished.

That said, I would like to thank my best friend of fifteen years Zig Sonnenburg, who supported me in more ways than I could count in this interesting adventure called life.

AnaLaura Arrelano, you helped my family so much and your generosity allowed to me to experience some of my most favorite of times! THANK YOU!

Parie Petty of www.WesternLithograpics.com THANK YOU!!! Her covers are AMAZING. As you can see by this cover she is immensely talented and is a wonderful human being and great businesswoman. Her LinkedIn profile is https://www.linkedin.com/in/pariepetty

Hossro Khorsand, who drew the Christ on the cover, THANK YOU!. His LinkedIn profile is https://www.linkedin.com/in/hossro-mir-k-khorsand-45b42157 and email ishosssro.graphics@icloud.com

To my beta readers, Dr. Eric Robins, Christopher Hinn and Marshall Belcher, thank you for your input!

Lastly, I would like to thank and acknowledge the OC Meditation Group (www.OCMeditationGroup.com). The wonderful group of people I have the honor and privilege to serve, "May you all achieve your Christhood in this lifetime!" You all inspire me to serve more and to achieve Christhood as soon as possible for the benefit of you and all sentient beings.

About the Author

Daniel O'Hara has lived a unique life, marching to the beat of his own internal drummer. Identifying more in the philosophy of the East, he developed a love of the martial arts at an early age. While searching for martial arts instructors, he realized there was much more to be learned. He then sought out the mystical teachings of the East and found Choa Kok Sui.

In 1987, at the young age of 19, he left UC Riverside and became a stockbroker. This was during the greed and glory days of Wall Street. He might have been the youngest stockbroker in Dean Witter's illustrious history. He experienced much pain, stress and some success. He became an expert in trading the commodity markets using the vibration of the planets and sacred geometry. This esoteric understanding of how vibration (energy) influences people, further pushed him to understand energy healing.

He has helped bring five companies public and even completed a billion-dollar transaction. He has experienced the highest of highs and the lowest of lows in the world of finance.

After five years in the industry and only in his mid-twenties, he fell apart from stress and looked to rebuild his physical, mental and emotional life. Little did he know at the time that these life lessons would send him on a quest to develop spiritually.

Finding the priceless teachings of Choa Kok Sui, Daniel was given the tools of self-development, sharing profound wisdom with, and healing others. Daniel has taught healing seminars in nine states and healed famous professional athletes from the NFL, NBA, MLB and UFC.

Daniel runs the www.OCMeditationGroup.com in Orange County, CA. He is very passionate about many causes including feeding/clothing the impoverished, working for animal rights, promoting sustainability issues and protecting the environment.

For more information about Daniel, his meditations and video seminars, please see www.DanielOHara.com, and www.ChristsCastle.com.

www.ingramcontent.com/pod-product-compliance
Lightning Source LLC
Chambersburg PA
CBHW070522130626
46555CB00003B/1307